DC SUPER HERO
FAIRY TALES

THE AMAZON PRINCESS AND THE PEA

by Laurie S. Sutton
ILLUSTRATED BY Agnes Garbowska
COLORS BY Sil Brys

WONDER WOMAN CREATED BY
WILLIAM MOULTON MARSTON

STONE ARCH BOOKS
a capstone imprint

Published by Stone Arch Books, an imprint of Capstone
1710 Roe Crest Drive, North Mankato, Minnesota 56003
capstonepub.com

Library of Congress Cataloging-in-Publication Data
Names: Sutton, Laurie, author. | Garbowska, Agnes, illustrator.
Title: The Amazon princess and the pea / by Laurie S. Sutton ; illustrated
by Agnes Garbowska.
Description: North Mankato, Minnesota : Stone Arch Books, an imprint of
Capstone, 2021. | Series: DC super hero fairy tales | Audience: Ages 8–11.
| Audience: Grades 4–6. | Summary: Wonder Woman recognizes that the
Beastiamorphs overrunning the island of Valdonia are creations of her old
enemy, Circe, so she sets out to deal with the threat; but she finds that the
petulant king wants Superman, Circe has disguised herself, and the only
clue is a strange, pea-sized stone hidden under a tower of mattresses on
Wonder Woman's bed—and she has to untangle Circe's spell, defeat the
sorceress, and prove to the king that she is a real hero.
Identifiers: LCCN 2021016028 (print) | LCCN 2021016029 (ebook) |
ISBN 9781663910639 (hardcover) | ISBN 9781663921413 (paperback) |
ISBN 9781663910608 (pdf)
Subjects: LCSH: Wonder Woman (Fictitious character)—Juvenile fiction.
| Circe (Mythological character)—Juvenile fiction. | Monsters—Juvenile
fiction. | Superheroes—Juvenile fiction. | Supervillains—Juvenile fiction.
| Fairy tales—Adaptations. | CYAC: Fairy tales. | Circe (Mythological
character)—Fiction. | Monsters—Fiction. | Superheroes—Fiction. |
Supervillains—Fiction. | LCGFT: Superhero fiction. | Fairy tales.
Classification: LCC PZ8.S92 Am 2021 (print) | LCC PZ8.S92 (ebook) |
DDC 813.54 [Fic]—dc23
LC record available at https://lccn.loc.gov/2021016028
LC ebook record available at https://lccn.loc.gov/2021016029

Designed by Hilary Wacholz

TABLE OF CONTENTS

ONCE UPON A TIME . . .

THE WORLD'S GREATEST
SUPER HEROES COLLIDED WITH
THE WORLD'S BEST-KNOWN
FAIRY TALES TO CREATE . . .

DC SUPER HERO
FAIRY TALES

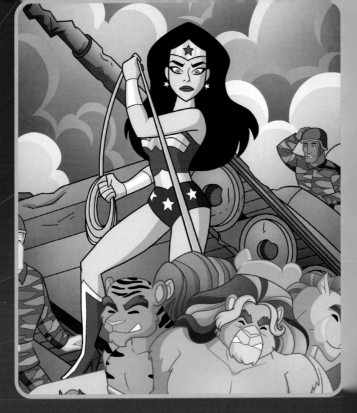

Now, Wonder Woman
must pass a secret nighttime
test and prove to doubters
that she's a real hero in
this twisted retelling of
"The Princess and the Pea."

Magic in the Air

Wonder Woman sat at a round table with the rest of her Justice League teammates. A meeting had been called at the Watchtower, their headquarters in orbit above Earth.

Behind the Amazon Princess, a large window revealed the curve of the planet below. Bright white clouds spread over the blues of the oceans and the browns and greens of the continents. It was the world that the Justice League had promised to protect.

Across from Wonder Woman, The Flash shifted in his seat and tapped his foot on the floor. Wonder Woman smiled to herself. The Fastest Man Alive could never keep still. Right next to her sat Batman. He was as silent as a statue. Superman stood at the head of the table. He was one of the most powerful people in the galaxy, but he was also the nicest person Wonder Woman had ever met.

"I call this meeting to order," Superman said. "The kingdom of Valdonia has sent us a message asking for help. It's a small island nation, but it seems to have a big problem."

The Man of Steel turned on a large screen. It showed images of a battle. Soldiers fought with giant creatures that were half-human and half-animal.

"Beastiamorphs!" Wonder Woman said.

"Beasty whats?" The Flash asked.

"*Beast-ee-a-morphs,*" Wonder Woman repeated slowly. "They're men who have been changed into beasts."

"They suddenly showed up on Valdonia and started to overrun the island," Superman said. "As you can see, the kingdom's forces are no match for the creatures."

The Justice League members watched the screen as the monsters tossed aside soldiers like dolls. They knocked over tanks like toys.

Wonder Woman stood up from the table and walked to the screen. She studied the images as if looking for something.

"I don't see her in the video, but where there are Beastiamorphs, Circe is not far away," Wonder Woman said. "They are creations of her magic."

"Circe, as in the sorceress of ancient Greek myth?" Superman asked.

"Isn't she a legend? Um, I mean myth. Or is it fairy tale?" The Flash asked. "I never could figure out the difference."

"Circe is neither myth nor legend, nor a fairy tale. She is very real," Wonder Woman replied. "We have clashed many times."

"I know. I created a Watchtower file on her," Batman said.

Batman pulled up a file from the Justice League data banks. The screen now showed a woman with long, dark hair dressed in a green and yellow costume. Purple energy crackled from her hands.

"Whoa! Immortal sorceress. Powers include spells, illusions, shape-shifting," The Flash read from the screen.

"I can handle Circe," Wonder Woman said. "I volunteer to go to Valdonia. I will rid them of the sorceress and her Beastiamorphs."

Superman nodded. "Good luck," he said.

Wonder Woman flew at super-speed to the kingdom of Valdonia. When she arrived, she found the island covered by a dome of thick, purple clouds. The clouds swirled like a hurricane. Purple energy bolts crackled through the storm like an electrified web.

There's nothing natural about this purple storm, Wonder Woman thought as she floated in the sky. *Circe must have put a magic shield over the island to stop anyone from helping the Valdonians. But the shield won't stop me.*

The Amazon Princess flew into the raging storm. As soon as she entered the clouds, she discovered they were not normal storm clouds. They were as thick as syrup and just as sticky. It was like moving through a lake of purple honey. She was quickly covered in goo.

Ugh. Circe's magic shield sure is messy! But if this goo is meant to keep me out or slow me down, it won't work, Wonder Woman thought.

Suddenly purple lightning struck out at the Amazon Princess. She reacted with super-speed and blocked the bolts with her bracelets.

KBAAM! BZAAAM!

Wonder Woman pushed through the thick, sticky clouds. The lightning seemed to follow her. She dodged the bolts when she could, and blocked them with her Amazon bracelets when she could not.

Finally, Wonder Woman clashed her bracelets together. They sent a massive wave of energy against the magical lightning.

BWAAAAM! CRAAACKLE!

The purple lightning stopped.

Wonder Woman flew down through the rest of the gooey, magical clouds and into clear air at last. She landed on the island, near a large building. It looked like a fairy-tale castle built for a theme park.

This must be the home of whoever sent the message for help, Wonder Woman decided.

Wonder Woman flew over to the massive front door. She looked down and saw she was covered in magical slime. Her hair was a tangled, dripping mess.

I am not going to make a good first impression, Wonder Woman thought.

The hero knocked on the door. But the door to the castle was large and thick. Wonder Woman had to use her fist and Amazon strength to make herself heard.

BOOOM! BOOOM! BOOOM!

No one answered. The Amazon Princess wondered if the people inside were afraid that it was Beastiamorphs pounding on the door. Then she saw a security camera mounted on the wall. Wonder Woman waved at it.

"Hello! I've come to help with your monster problem!" Wonder Woman shouted at the camera. "The Justice League sent me!"

A moment later the door swung open to reveal a grand entrance hall. It was filled with statues, paintings, and wall hangings worthy of a royal palace.

Wonder Woman stepped inside and came face-to-face with a line of soldiers. They stood in front of an older man dressed in a green and yellow uniform that was heavily decorated with gold braid and medals. He glared at Wonder Woman as if she were an enemy.

"I am General Hans," the officer said.

"I am Princess Diana of Themyscira," Wonder Woman said. "Also known as—"

"Wonder Woman. Yes, I know who you are," the general said with a deep frown. "The famous Super Hero. You don't look like much of one right now."

Wonder Woman tried to shrug off the comment, but her shoulders were stiff from the purple goo that was slowly drying on her body. Her hair was starting to feel like straw.

"What I look like doesn't matter," Wonder Woman said. "What's important is I can help you get rid of the beasts that have overrun the kingdom."

"We'll see about that," the general said. "Come with me. King Bernard and Prince Erwin wish to speak with you."

CHAPTER 2

First Impressions

General Hans turned and started to walk out of the entrance hall. Wonder Woman followed. The soldiers fell in step behind the Amazon Princess. They marched through halls richly decorated with art treasures and portraits of royal family members.

General Hans led Wonder Woman into the palace throne room. But the Super Hero quickly saw it was now also being used as a war room to track Beastiamorph battles.

Military officers crowded around a giant table with maps and a large battlefield model. The Amazon Princess noticed that the model showed very few soldiers left out on the field.

Wonder Woman walked past the officers and stepped toward the center of the room. There, the king sat on a grand throne sparkling with precious jewels. Medals and gold braid covered his bright green jacket. The crown on his head was very fancy.

"Your Royal Highness, King Bernard, sir! I bring you Princess Diana of Themyscira, Wonder Woman of the Justice League!" General Hans announced.

The general walked away from Wonder Woman and left her standing alone to face all the men in the room.

"Wonder Woman?" the king shouted, jumping up from his throne. The fancy crown almost fell off his head. "The Justice League sent Wonder Woman? Where is Superman? He's the *real* Super Hero!"

The military officers stopped what they were doing as soon as the king raised his voice. They looked first at the king, and then at Wonder Woman. Then back at the king.

"I wanted Superman!" King Bernard said. "That was supposed to be in the video! Erwin! You were responsible for the video!"

"It was in there, Father!" Prince Erwin said as he marched up to the king.

Wonder Woman was sure that such a request was *not* in the video she had viewed on the Watchtower, but she said nothing.

Prince Erwin also wore a green and yellow uniform and had a crown. But it was not as large or as fancy as his father's.

"Superman was . . . not available," Wonder Woman said. "But I can help you. I know what the creatures are and how to defeat them."

"How do you know what the monsters are?" Prince Erwin asked.

"I know because I've fought them before," Wonder Woman said. "They are creatures of magic, created by the sorceress Circe."

"Magic? Sorceress? There's no such thing!" General Hans declared. "That's nonsense."

The general started to laugh. Then the king started to laugh. Then Prince Erwin started to laugh. Soon all the military officers in the war room were laughing.

Wonder Woman patiently waited for the uproar to pass. At last the room fell quiet, and the Amazon Princess was able to speak.

"I have seen many incredible things as a member of the Justice League," Wonder Woman said. "I have seen magic and monsters that can destroy worlds. I have fought next to Earth's greatest Super Heroes. But if you do not want my help, I will leave."

General Hans hoped that the Amazon Princess would leave. This was because the general had a secret. He was really the Super-Villain Circe in disguise!

Circe had turned the real general into a Beastiamorph days ago. Then she had used her shape-shifting powers to take his form. This way she could take control of the army and cause maximum chaos.

Also, Circe liked watching the men run around the war room like chickens in a panic.

Of all the Super Heroes the Justice League could send, why did it have to be Wonder Woman! Circe thought. *She is my archenemy!*

"No, you may stay," King Bernard said with a sigh. "General Hans, show Wonder Woman to a guest room. She needs to clean up. She's dripping on my floor."

"I am ready to face the Beastiamorphs now," Wonder Woman said. "My appearance has nothing to do with my battle skills."

"That's up to the general," the king replied and paid no more attention to the hero.

"You can wait until morning," General Hans said as he turned to leave the throne room. "It's night and the monsters don't come out after dark."

"Why not?" Wonder Woman asked as she followed him.

Because I don't feel like it! Circe thought. *I came to this little island to play. The men here are so self-important, it's fun to turn them into slobbering, mindless beasts. But there are more relaxing ways to spend an evening besides laying waste to the kingdom.*

General Hans shrugged. "The people of Valdonia are just glad for the break."

The general led Wonder Woman to one of the guest rooms. It was full of art and statues just like the rest of the palace.

What really stood out, though, was the huge four-poster bed. It was piled high with mattresses and thick feather quilts. It was so tall that a small ladder was needed to get to the top.

"That's a lot of mattresses," Wonder Woman said.

"The king wants his guests to be comfortable," General Hans replied. He pointed to a golden door. "The bathroom is in there. It has a very large tub. You should use it."

The general left before Wonder Woman could say thank you. The Amazon Princess looked down at her slime-covered body.

"A bath might be a good idea," Wonder Woman said and went into the bathroom.

General Hans stood outside the guest room and looked around to make sure no one else was in the hallway. Then he suddenly disappeared in a swirl of purple mist. He reappeared in a secret lair thousands of miles away from Valdonia.

But now he was not General Hans.
Circe stood in her true form.

I have to find a way to keep Wonder Woman from fighting my Beastiamorphs, Circe thought. *There must be a way to make her leave.*

The sorceress looked through shelves of spell books and scrolls. She picked up bottles of potions and then tossed them aside.

At last she found an object that made her smile an evil smile. She picked up a small purple stone no larger than a pea.

Ah! This Dream Stone will do the trick, Circe thought. *It's a piece of the Gate of Ivory from the realm of Hypnos, god of sleep. I can use it to send dreams to Wonder Woman—nightmares that will convince her she cannot beat my Beastiamorphs. She will give up her mission and leave Valdonia for good.*

Circe clutched the stone in her fist and transported back to the palace. She secretly slipped into Wonder Woman's room.

The villain tucked the Dream Stone under the big bed's many mattresses while the Amazon Princess was in the bathroom.

"Pleasant dreams," Circe whispered with a smile.

CHAPTER 3

Not-So-Pleasant Dreams

Wonder Woman walked out of the bathroom wearing a fluffy robe. She was feeling clean and refreshed.

Soaking in the tub had washed away the goo from Circe's magical cloud. Getting it off her costume had taken extra scrubbing, but the Lasso of Truth stayed bright and glowing. The special rope was made by the Greek god Hephaestus. It was not affected by Circe's magic.

Wonder Woman climbed up onto the tall bed. She stretched out and made herself comfortable.

There's nothing wrong with getting a little rest before I battle the Beastiamorphs, Wonder Woman thought. *However, I should watch out for Circe's tricks. General Hans said the Beastiamorphs don't attack at night, but that doesn't mean Circe won't.*

Wonder Woman did not plan to fall asleep, but she dozed off as soon as her head touched the pillow. Hidden under all the layers of the bed, the Dream Stone started to glow.

The Amazon Princess dreamed . . .

∽ ∾

Wonder Woman stood in a field beneath a purple sky. The meadow was empty—except for a charging mass of Beastiamorphs!

They ran toward her on human legs but snarled with animal mouths. Some had the heads of lions and tigers. Many were part bull. Others were part bear.

Circe floated above the mass. She was dressed in her green and yellow Super-Villain costume. Purple energy crackled around her.

"My pets will destroy you, Wonder Woman!" Circe shouted.

"I have beaten them—and you—before, Circe!" Wonder Woman declared.

"We'll see about that," Circe replied.

The Amazon Princess raced toward the horde. She took the Lasso of Truth from her belt and twirled it above her head as she ran.

SWOOOSH! SWOOOSH!

Wonder Woman tossed the Lasso over a group of Beastiamorphs. It dropped around their shoulders. Wonder Woman tugged the Lasso tight with a twist of her wrist. It pulled the creatures together in a bunch.

"Surrender," Wonder Woman commanded the Beastiamorphs within the Lasso.

SNAAP! SNAAP!

Suddenly the Beastiamorphs broke free from the Lasso. It had snapped as if it was an ordinary rope. Wonder Woman was shocked.

"That's impossible!" the Amazon Princess gasped. "The power of the Lasso should have made them obey!"

The mass of Beastiamorphs ran toward Wonder Woman. Soon she was buried under their hooves and paws and claws.

Wonder Woman used her amazing Amazon strength to shove her way out from the swarm. She flew into the air, but the Beastiamorphs paid no attention to her. They were racing toward a small farming village.

I have to stop them before they destroy that town, Wonder Woman thought. She started to fly toward the village.

A bolt of purple energy struck Wonder Woman. She dropped out of the sky.

THUUUD!

Wonder Woman hit the ground and rolled. She got to her feet a moment later and saw Circe flying above her.

"You can't save them," Circe said. "You are a failure, not a hero."

Wonder Woman ignored the villain. She started to run toward the village.

But Wonder Woman could not use her Amazon speed. She could barely move her legs. All she could do was watch as the Beastiamorphs destroyed the village.

"You are a failure!" Circe shouted again. She landed in front of her archenemy. "No wonder the king wanted Superman, not you."

Wonder Woman fought to break free from whatever invisible magic was holding her back. It was no use.

"Give up. You're not a hero," Circe said. "You never were a hero. I'll show you what you really are."

Circe waved her hands. A ball of purple magic surrounded the Amazon Princess.

When the energy faded away, Wonder Woman was no longer human. She was a small bunny rabbit!

"Ha, ha! Your true self is finally revealed," Circe said. "You're a small, frightened creature that hides in a hole at the first sign of danger."

Wonder Woman looked down at her fluffy new form and big bunny feet. They made her feel weird and awkward. But she still wore her Super Hero costume and Amazon bracelets. That gave her confidence. The Amazon Princess adjusted her tiara to better fit over her long ears.

"You are too cute as a little bunny," Circe said with a laugh. "Maybe I should turn you into a frog instead."

Wonder Woman leaped up at Circe. She used her powerful back feet to land a karate kick on the sorceress.

THWUUUMP!

Circe cried out as she fell backward and landed on the ground. Wonder Woman bounced onto Circe's chest and stared down at her foe.

"I might have the body of a bunny, but I am still a hero!" Wonder Woman declared. "Nothing will ever change that."

Wonder Woman suddenly awoke. She sat up in the tall bed and was surprised to see that it was morning. A loud knocking was coming at the door.

KNOCK! KNOCK! KNOCK!

I must have been dreaming! Wonder Woman realized. *Of course, being a bunny should have been a clue.*

"Wonder Woman! The king summons you!" a voice said from outside the door.

"I will be right there," the Super Hero replied.

That was a troubling dream, Wonder Woman thought. *I couldn't seem to defeat Circe or the Beastiamorphs.* But the details of the dream were already fading away. All that remained was an uneasy feeling.

Wonder Woman jumped down from the bed. That's when her keen Amazon eyesight noticed something strange about the bottom layer of mattresses.

There's a lump, Wonder Woman thought.

The Amazon Princess lifted the stack of mattresses with one hand. A small object rested on the bottom mattress. It looked like a purple stone pea.

What is this? Wonder Woman thought as she picked up Circe's Dream Stone. It glowed softly. *It feels like magic.*

KNOCK! KNOCK! KNOCK!

"Coming!" Wonder Woman called.

Wonder Woman quickly tucked the small stone into her belt. The hero opened the door and saw a nervous soldier.

"Please! His Majesty wants you in the war room immediately!" the young man said.

"Then I won't keep him waiting," Wonder Woman replied.

The Amazon Princess zoomed away down the palace corridor at super-speed. The soldier was left behind with his mouth open in amazement.

CHAPTER 4

Secret Sorcery

Wonder Woman sped into the war room. King Bernard sat on his golden throne. Prince Erwin stood nearby while General Hans whispered something in the king's ear. The king looked at Wonder Woman and frowned.

Wonder Woman could only imagine what the general had said. *Nothing good, I'm sure,* she thought. *Why is the general trying to make trouble for me? I'm here to help.*

The Amazon Princess walked straight up to the throne. She looked and felt like her normal, Super Hero self now that she was not covered in magical slime.

"Good morning," Wonder Woman said politely. "You wanted to see me?"

"Yes," the king replied. "General Hans needs to brief you on today's plan of attack."

"I hope you are well rested and up to the task," the general said. "How did you sleep?"

"Not very well, actually," Wonder Woman said. "I had a bad dream."

Disguised as General Hans, Circe tried not to smile. *Good! That's exactly what the Dream Stone was supposed to do,* she thought. *I hope the dream was bad enough to shake you up and make you leave this island.*

"I don't usually have nightmares," Wonder Woman said. "So I wonder if they were caused by what I found under my bed."

The Amazon Princess pulled the little purple stone out of her belt.

"You felt *that* under all the mattresses?" King Bernard gasped in surprise.

"In a way, yes," Wonder Woman replied.

"It's the size of a pea! I'm impressed!" the king said. "Only royalty with our superior senses could have felt such a small thing!"

Wonder Woman tried not to roll her eyes. "Well, I did tell you that I'm an Amazon Princess," she said.

"Then you are one of us, Princess Wonder Woman!" the king declared. He jumped up from his throne and took her by the arm. "I will show you the battle plan myself!"

King Bernard led Wonder Woman over to a large table covered with maps of Valdonia. Prince Erwin and General Hans followed. The general had an intense frown on his face.

Grrr! The Dream Stone failed me. And how did she even find it? Circe thought. *This is bad. Its magic could lead back to me!*

King Bernard proudly showed Wonder Woman the maps of his kingdom. Forests stood to the east of the palace. To the west were grasslands and fields of crops. A few villages were scattered here and there.

"Hmm. Where could Circe be hiding?" Wonder Woman said. "Valdonia isn't large. You would think she'd be easy to find."

"Why do you speak of this Circe?" the king asked. "It's the monsters that are causing all the trouble."

"Because Circe is the one turning Valdonia's men into Beastiamorphs and sending them out to cause destruction. She thinks it's fun," Wonder Woman replied.

"That is pure fantasy. There's no such thing as sorceresses," General Hans scoffed.

"Circe is real," Wonder Woman said. "And she is somewhere on this island."

The Amazon Princess held up the small stone. She stared at it as if trying to see into a crystal ball.

"My dream . . . it's coming back to me now," Wonder Woman said. "I saw Circe. She led an army of Beastiamorph monsters. I failed to defeat them."

"Maybe the dream was trying to tell you something," General Hans muttered.

"Was it a prophecy?" King Bernard asked.

"No, but this stone is magic. I think Circe used it to get into my dreams and mess with my head," Wonder Woman said. "Which means she put it under my bed. She was in the palace."

"A sorceress was in my palace?" King Bernard shouted in alarm.

"There's no such thing as sorceresses!" General Hans yelled, but it was too late.

Panic broke out in the war room. Soldiers rushed to protect their king. The military officers turned around and around looking for an intruder. Everyone shouted orders.

Wonder Woman stood like a pillar in the middle of the confusion. She took the Lasso of Truth and twirled it above her head.

SWOOOSH! SWOOOSH! SWOOOSH!

"Everyone, be calm!" Wonder Woman said as the golden cord blazed with light.

The war room fell quiet. Even General Hans was silent. Wonder Woman stopped twirling the Lasso and looped it over one hand. She held the purple stone in the other.

"The Lasso of Truth can track magic," Wonder Woman said. "All I have to do is touch it to the stone. It will reveal the trail of magic that connects the stone to Circe."

"If you say a sorceress is behind all this, I believe you, Princess Wonder Woman," the king said.

Wonder Woman moved the glowing stone toward the Lasso of Truth.

No! I can't be revealed! Circe thought. *I need a distraction. I think it's time to unleash my Beastiamorphs.*

All eyes were on Wonder Woman and King Bernard. No one noticed General Hans make a small gesture. No one saw the sparks of purple energy leap from his fingertips.

Suddenly a soldier seated at the radio receiver shouted to the king. "Your Majesty! Outposts five and six report that monsters are coming out of the Eastern Forest," he said.

All the officers began running to their battle stations in the war room.

I might not need the Lasso of Truth to find Circe after all, Wonder Woman thought. *She's probably leading the Beastiamorph attack.*

The Amazon Princess put the purple stone back in her belt.

"I'll take care of those monsters," Wonder Woman told the king. "It's what I came here to do."

CHAPTER 5

BEASTLY BATTLE

Wonder Woman left the war room in a blur of super-speed. She ran out of the palace and leaped into the sky. The swirling magic storm still spun high above the island. The purple clouds turned the sunlight passing through them into shades of violet.

Wonder Woman flew over the countryside toward the battlefield. From above, she could see tanks leading the attack. Troops followed behind in orderly ranks.

But the ranks fell apart when the human army met the Beastiamorphs. The creatures washed over everything like a wave.

There's at least a thousand Beastiamorphs! Circe must have transformed almost all of the men on Valdonia! Wonder Woman thought. *But where is she? I thought she would be leading the attack.*

The Amazon Princess swooped down out of the sky like a hawk. She plowed through the front line of Beastiamorphs. The giant creatures were tossed into the air and crashed into each other.

That did not stop the Beastiamorphs. They got up and started fighting again. Wonder Woman saw the monsters charge toward a group of soldiers defending a smashed tank.

The soldiers are no match against the Beastiamorphs, Wonder Woman thought. *But I am.*

THWOOOMP!

The Amazon Princess landed between the soldiers and the Beastiamorphs. The impact shook the ground. The Beastiamorphs paused, surprised by Wonder Woman's sudden arrival.

Wonder Woman took the Lasso of Truth from her belt and twirled it above her head.

SWOOOSH! SWOOOSH!

She tossed the Lasso over the group of Beastiamorphs. It dropped around their shoulders. Wonder Woman tugged the Lasso tight with a twist of her wrist. It pulled the creatures together in a bunch.

Wait! This is familiar! Wonder Woman thought. *Now I remember. This was in my dream!*

An image of the Lasso snapping flashed in her mind. She remembered feeling defeated.

No. That was a false dream sent by Circe, Wonder Woman thought. *But this is real life.*

"Surrender," Wonder Woman commanded the Beastiamorphs within the Lasso. They obeyed.

The Valdonian soldiers rushed forward to attack.

"No! Don't hurt them!" Wonder Woman said. "These creatures are actually your friends! Look, they are wearing Valdonian clothes and uniforms."

It took a moment for the soldiers to realize that what Wonder Woman said was true. They read some of the name tags on the ripped uniforms.

"That's Captain Muller!" one of the soldiers said. "We thought he was lost in the first wave."

"*All* of these creatures are people you know. They have been transformed by . . . powerful forces," Wonder Woman said. She did not want to argue the existence of magic in the middle of a battlefield. "Just keep an eye on them until they can get back to normal."

Wonder Woman freed the Beastiamorphs from the Lasso of Truth. The soldiers stepped back nervously. But the creatures sat down on the ground and did not move.

The Amazon Princess launched into the air. She looked out over the battlefield, but she could not spot Circe.

Where is Circe? Wonder Woman thought. *She usually shows up to take credit for all the chaos she causes.*

Wonder Woman landed back on the battlefield and used her Lasso to round up more Beastiamorphs. They were innocent victims of Circe. The Amazon Princess wanted to capture them, not fight them. That did not stop the creatures from trying to harm her.

A swarm of Beastiamorphs attacked Wonder Woman from behind. They tore at her with claws and talons, but the Amazon's skin was almost as tough as Superman's. They did not leave a mark.

Wonder Woman used her super-strength
to lift the monsters up over her head in a ball
of waving arms and legs. Then she tossed the
mass into a nearby lake.

That should dampen their desire to fight,
Wonder Woman thought.

Another group of Beastiamorphs charged
toward the Amazon Princess.

*I can't save the Valdonians by fighting the
Beastiamorphs one swarm at a time,* Wonder
Woman decided. *I have to end the fighting all
at once. Then I can focus on finding Circe and
defeating the cause of this problem!*

Wonder Woman looped one end of
the Lasso of Truth around the nearest
Beastiamorph. Holding the Lasso's other
end, she ran at super-speed around both
the monster horde and the Valdonian army.

The Lasso stretched and stretched. Soon, everyone was wrapped up in the bright, glowing cord.

"Stop fighting!" Wonder Woman told the soldiers and Beastiamorphs.

Everyone obeyed.

"Circe, reveal yourself!" Wonder Woman ordered.

Nothing happened. There was no sign of the sorceress.

Well, that only means she's not within the circle of the Lasso of Truth, Wonder Woman thought. *So where is she?*

The Amazon Princess knew there was still a way to find out. She took the little purple stone from her belt. She touched it to the glowing Lasso.

"Lead me to Circe," Wonder Woman commanded.

A tendril of magical energy curled up and out of the stone. It rose into the air and paused. Then it sped like a spear to the west.

"No fighting!" Wonder Woman reminded the Beastiamorphs and Valdonian soldiers as she released them from the Lasso. Then she flew off to follow the magical energy trail.

Wonder Woman was surprised when it brought her to the royal palace. *Oh no. It's leading to the throne room,* she realized.

The Amazon Princess flew into the throne room. The tendril of magical energy had formed a spiral above General Hans. The purple spiral looked just like the larger swirl of clouds above the island.

"General Hans! You are Circe!" Wonder Woman shouted.

"Yes!" the general admitted. "And you've ruined my fun with the Valdonians. For that, I will destroy you!"

A blaze of purple light covered General Hans as the furious sorceress used her shape-shifting powers. When the light faded, the general was gone. In his place stood a snarling dragon!

The king, prince, and all the military officers ran away from the threat. Wonder Woman raced straight for it. She twirled the Lasso of Truth. The dragon started to suck in air for a blast of fiery breath, but the Super Hero was too fast. With a flick of her wrist, Wonder Woman tossed the Lasso and quickly snared the dragon around its neck.

"Surrender, Circe, and return to your human form!" Wonder Woman commanded.

A flash of light filled the room. The dragon changed into a woman with dark hair wearing a green and yellow costume.

"You were right about the sorceress!" King Bernard said, peeking out of his hiding place.

"Circe, turn all the Beastiamorphs back to their human forms," Wonder Woman said.

"I . . . I must obey," Circe grumbled. Purple energy crackled around her.

Out on the battlefield, the magical energy began to surround the Beastiamorphs.

"Your Highness! Messages are coming in from the battlefield!" said the soldier at the radio receiver. "They report that the monsters are turning back into our men!"

The king walked over and gave a small bow. "Thank you, Wonder Woman," he said. "I am glad you came. You have proven to be a true hero."

"And she's a princess!" Prince Erwin declared. He raced over and grasped Wonder Woman's hands in his. "I want you to be my royal wife. You must marry me!"

"I don't know if that was a request or a demand. But my answer is no, thank you," Wonder Woman replied. "Now, my mission here is done."

Wonder Woman left the palace with the captive Circe. The sky above the island was a clear blue. The swirling clouds were gone. Wonder Woman launched into the air. She left Valdonia behind to live her life happily ever after . . . at least until the next amazing mission.

THE ORIGINAL STORY:
THE PRINCESS AND THE PEA

Once upon a time, a prince searched for a princess to marry, but she had to be a *real* princess. He looked far and wide, but none of the women he met lived up to his idea of what a real princess should be.

One stormy night, a loud knock pounded at the front door of the palace. A young woman stood outside, soaking wet from the rain. She was brought before the prince and his parents, the king and queen.

When the young woman said that she was a real princess, the queen did not believe her. With her wet clothing and dripping hair, she certainly did not look like a princess! The queen decided to test her.

The queen secretly went to a bedroom and put a small pea under the mattress on the bed. Then she piled twenty more mattresses and thick feather quilts on top of it. There, the princess was invited to sleep.

The next morning, the queen asked the young woman how she had slept. The woman replied she had slept very badly. Something hard in the bed had caused bruises all over her! The queen was convinced at last. Only a real princess would be sensitive enough to feel such a tiny pea under all the mattresses. The princess had passed the test.

The prince married the princess, and they lived happily ever after. And the pea? It was put into a museum, where it remains to this day.

SUPERPOWERED TWISTS

- The original princess travels through a rainstorm to get to the palace, and the royal family isn't impressed by her soggy appearance. Wonder Woman flies through a magical storm shield and looks less than heroic because she's covered in slimy, purple goo!

- The pea in the original tale is an actual vegetable. In this story, the tiny object is a magical stone.

- In the fairy tale, the queen secretly tests the princess by putting the pea under the mattress. In this story, Circe tests Wonder Woman in her dreams and tries to make the hero doubt her amazing abilities.

- At the end of the fairy tale, the queen believes the young woman is a real princess after she senses the pea. At the end of this story, the king finally accepts Wonder Woman as a true hero after she saves the entire kingdom from a monster horde and an evil sorceress!

- No marriages here. Wonder Woman turns down the prince's proposal and flies off to her next mission.

TALK ABOUT IT

1. The king was not very impressed with Wonder Woman when she first came to the palace. Has anyone ever judged you before they got to know you? How did that make you feel? How do you think Wonder Woman felt?

2. Were you surprised that General Hans was actually Circe in disguise? Why or why not?

3. Talk about the ways Wonder Woman showed she was a real Super Hero. Use examples from the story to back up your answer.

WRITE ABOUT IT

1. Think of the saying, "Don't judge a book by its cover." Write two paragraphs about how it connects to this story.

2. Real heroes don't always have superpowers. Write about a hero in your life. Describe how they are special and why you think of them as a hero.

3. Fairy tales are often told and retold over many generations, and the details can change depending on who tells them. Write your version of "The Princess and the Pea" story. Change a lot or a little, but make it your own!

THE AUTHOR

Laurie S. Sutton has been reading comics since she was a kid. She grew up to become an editor for Marvel, DC Comics, Starblaze, and Tekno Comics. She has written Adam Strange for DC, Star Trek: Voyager for Marvel, plus Star Trek: Deep Space Nine and Witch Hunter for Malibu Comics. There are long boxes of comics in her closet where there should be clothing and shoes. Laurie has lived all over the world and currently resides in Florida.

THE ILLUSTRATORS

Agnes Garbowska is an artist who has worked with many major book publishers, illustrating such brands as DC Super Hero Girls, Teen Titans Go!, My Little Pony, and Care Bears. She was born in Poland and came to Canada at a young age. Being an only child, she escaped into a world of books, cartoons, and comics. She currently lives in the United States and enjoys sharing her office with her two little dogs.

Sil Brys is a colorist and graphic designer. She has worked on many comics and children's books, having had fun coloring stories for Teen Titans Go!, Scooby-Doo, Tom & Jerry, Looney Tunes, DC Super Hero Girls, Care Bears, and more. She lives in a small village in Argentina, where her home is also her office. She loves to create there, surrounded by forests, mountains, and a lot of books.

archenemy (arch-EH-nuh-mee)—a person's main enemy

defeat (dih-FEET)—to win over someone or something else

distraction (dih-STRAK-shuhn)—something that takes focus away from other things

horde (HORD)—a large, unorganized group

lair (LAIR)—a secret, hidden place

overrun (oh-ver-RUN)—to spread throughout and take over a place with a large number of people or things

reveal (rih-VEEL)—to show something clearly, often for the first time or after being hidden

shape-shift (SHEYP-shift)—to change one's body and looks completely

sorceress (SOR-suh-ress)—a woman with magical powers

tendril (TEN-druhl)—something that looks like a long, twisting plant stem

transform (trans-FORM)—to change something completely

war room (WAR ROOM)—a room where military leaders plan and keep track of battles